Amie's House is the author's second book. Her debut novel *Ruhelose Seelen – Kann ein Verfluchter jemals glücklich sein?* was published in German in 2018 (ISBN: 978-3748108917). An English translation is in progress.

Ilona Galvagni

Amie's House

Psychological thriller

German National Library bibliographic
information:
This publication is listed in the The German
National Library's German National
Bibliography; detailed bibliographic data is
available online on dnb.dnb.de.

Production and publication:
BoD – Books on Demand, Norderstedt, Germany

ISBN: 9783754300565

For my Welsh friends Julie and Amie whose childhood memories of their haunted house inspired me to this book and who are happy for me to use their names in it.*

Done! What a relief! Julie straightened up, wiped her hands on her jeans and rubbed her aching back. The last cardboard box was unpacked, the last cupboard stocked with crockery. Finally the move was complete.

She cast an approving look around the old-fashioned but quite spacious kitchen. Her very own kitchen in her new home. The manor had been built in 1901 and she had unexpectedly inherited it from a great-aunt of whose existence she had not had the faintest idea. She considered it a bit of an exaggeration to call the house a manor. It was a large house and definitely very old but she didn't find it very impressive. Anyway, that was its name. Maenor Tywyll. Welsh for »Dark Manor«. She found the name a bit creepy and tried not to think too much about why it may have been given it all those years ago. It was definitely dark and also a bit gloomy, both inside and out.

As she was always strapped for cash, she moved in right away instead of refurbishing or modernising anything first. As long as she could save the expensive rent for her city apartment, the renovations could wait.

So here she would live now, in the small village of Gwyllin, somewhere in the middle of nowhere in the most northerly part of Wales. In a small valley, surrounded by rough nature and high mountains. She would have to get used to that. After having lived in a tiny and very overpriced apartment in the centre of Cardiff, the capital of Wales, this was a huge change.

Being a freelance translator, luckily she could work from anywhere in the world as long as she had an internet connection. Conversely, this meant that she could not work initially as this ramshackle pile didn't even have a telephone line, let alone Wi-Fi. She had not considered this fact and when it finally occurred to her, she had already terminated the lease of her tiny studio apartment in Cardiff. She may have been a bit rash and impulsive there once again, as she often was. The prospect of her own big house embedded in a romantic landscape had simply been too overwhelming.

Oh well. Now she'd saved the rent but had no income either. She could only hope that she would soon be provided with telephone and an internet connection. At least she had applied for it.

She jolted from her thoughts when she heard a clank behind her. She turned and sighed when she spotted the old rusty soup ladle lying on the floor. Siyah seemed to behave as badly here as she had behaved in Cardiff, only that this house offered her much more space and the possibility for mischief. She'd rather not think about this yet.

She had taken in Siyah, her old pitch-black cat, as a kitten after her mother had been run over by a car. She had spent many a night nursing and bottle feeding the kitten. Fortunately, the tiny cat had survived and Julie had named her Siyah as according to her research that was the Turkish word for »black«.

Julie adored her. It always annoyed her, however, that the cat did not care at all about the fact that she was, in theory, banned from walking and sitting on the kitchen counter and table. She did it anyway. Sometimes Julie even felt like she did it on purpose because she knew she was not allowed to. Siyah was 13 years old and if she hadn't learnt it by now, she never would. Julie was resigned to that. The cat simply was more pigheaded than herself. There was nothing to be done about it.

One moment later, Siyah came strolling into the kitchen with her head held high, loudly meowing for her dinner. Right, her food was long overdue. Julie had been so busy with unpacking the boxes and stocking the cupboards that she had lost track of time. As soon as she had filled Siyah's bowl with her nightly ration of food and put it on the floor, the cat came running up excitedly and started eating happily while purring loudly.

»Enjoy. I hope you like it. Your first meal in our new home. « Julie said and lovingly petted the cat's dark fur.

Julie stretched and yawned. She should eat something herself. After this long relocation day she was starving but she was way too tired to take on that antiquated monstrosity of a cooker. She would postpone that challenge to tomorrow. For today, all she wanted was sleep.

Somewhat exhausted, she climbed the creaky old wooden staircase leading to the upper floor. The last thing that crossed her mind before she fell sleep was that she would have to renovate that staircase.

Julie opened her eyes, confused and caught in a state somewhere between sleep and being awake. It was pitch-dark around her, so it had to be the middle of the night. She had neither closed the worm-eaten wooden shutters nor the moth-eaten curtains before going to bed and yet not the slightest ray of light entered her bedroom.

Why had she woken? She listened to the silence and heard nothing. Oh well, back to sleep. Julie nestled back down in the worn mattress, pulling the way too thick blanket up to her nose. Suddenly she heard it again. The noise that must have woken her. It sounded like….footsteps. Heavy, shuffling irregular footsteps. And they seemed to come from above. From the ceiling.

What was up there? Nothing but the attic. Had someone broken in and was searching the old attic for valuables? That was possible. The house looked a bit run-down from the outside and had stood empty for a long time. There were no direct neighbours and it was highly likely that nobody had noticed that someone had moved in. Maybe some youngsters were using her attic as their nightly den?

Should she call the police? Oh, damn! She couldn't. A bit difficult without landline or mobile phone signal. Swearing under her breath, she switched on the bedside lamp – a hideous fringed thing made of a fabric that had once likely been white but had long since yellowed. She swung her legs out of bed, put on her slippers and, wrapped up in the fluffy dressing gown she had laid out for the coming morning, she opened the bedroom door as quietly as possible and listened. She heard nothing for a moment, then the footsteps resumed their walk across the attic.

What should she do? She would have to check who was up there but she didn't have the courage to do it. What if the burglar was armed? She returned to the bedroom, looking for a suitable weapon. The fire irons next to the old fireplace caught her eye. She grabbed the poker and almost collapsed under its unexpectedly heavy weight. Gosh, was it made of cast iron? She held it with both hands and slinked back out into the corridor where she paused until her eyes got used to the darkness. She could not switch on the lights after all, unless she wanted to warn the burglar.

With bated breath she tiptoed towards the dusty staircase leading to the attic and climbed it, placing her feet slowly and carefully, worrying that the decayed wood might break or at least creak. Luckily, neither happened. At the upper end of the staircase there was another door. It was closed but she could hear the shuffling steps behind it, even louder now. They were definitely coming from there.

Julie took a deep breath before she pushed open the door with a jerk and shouted out: »Who's there?« The steps stopped abruptly. She expected someone to run towards and past her, perhaps trying to knock her down or overpower her, but nothing happened at all. There was nothing but silence.

With clenched teeth Julie groped about for the light switch on the wall next to the door until she eventually found it. A single dusty bulb lit the attic with dim half-light. Or, strictly speaking, with shadows rather than light. And those shadows were bloody ghostly. Even more so as the attic seemed huge. Julie's spirit broke. What could she do alone against a potentially aggressive intruder hiding somewhere in the shadows or behind the boxes? She was only 159 centimetres tall and rather petite. Her arms were already shaking under the weight of the poker which she could only just hold. Was she trying to fool herself? She stood no chance. So she changed her strategy.

»Listen, whoever you are. You probably didn't know that someone lives in this house. I'll give you an opportunity to leave my house immediately, otherwise I'll have to call the police!« she shouted into the darkness and tried her hardest to make her voice sound firm, determined and fearless. In truth she was scared witless. She ran back to her bedroom as fast as she could. She would have been a lot faster without the poker but leaving it behind was, of course, not an option. Further arming whoever it was made no sense.

Back in the bedroom she turned the key twice and blocked the doorknob with the poker. She looked around the room, searching, until her glance fell on the small chest of drawers. She made a beeline for it and, with all her might, pushed it in front of the door to barricade it further. She scratched the beautiful old wooden floor with the rhombic pattern in the process but did not care.

Heart pounding, she pressed into a corner of the room and listened. She couldn't hear the steps anymore but didn't believe anyone had come down the stairs from the attic either. Surely she would have heard that? Maybe not. After all she had made a lot of noise moving the drawers and hadn't paid attention to any noises from the staircase. She could only hope that the person – whoever it may have been –

had taken her half-hearted warning seriously and run off.

After listening for a few more minutes that seemed like ages but not hearing anything she returned to bed. This time she pulled the blanket over her head entirely. Should there still be someone in the house, she would rather not know. That someone was welcome to take whatever they wanted from the attic. She doubted that there was anything of value up there. Probably nothing but old books, suitcases and broken furniture rotting away. She was fine with them having those if it made them happy. As long as they didn't harm her and Siyah.

There was no more hope for restful sleep that night but shortly before dawn mere exhaustion sent her into a restless doze.

It was already light outside when Julie woke up the next morning, **or** as light as it gets on a typical rainy Welsh November day. Dark enough to leave the electric light on all day. »Depressing weather!« Julie mumbled as she dragged herself from bed with severe back pain caused by the fact that a spiral spring had pierced the mattress. She would have to replace so many things in this house, almost everything. The only question was how she would pay for it all. Her shopping list would be extensive. A new mattress was definitely first on the list.

Julie automatically reached out for the dressing gown, as she did every morning, but today she grasped into thin air. She hadn't taken it off after her flight from the attic but had slept in it. She had only shaken her slippers off her feet, which meant that she now had to stoop down, one hand pressed on her aching lower back, in order to put them on. As she did so, her gaze lingered on the bedside lamp and she stopped short. She was pretty sure she hadn't switched it off but still it was switched off. Maybe the bulb had gone? Or maybe power was off right now. That wouldn't come as a shock. In fact she was rather surprised that the old wiring in this house worked at all and that she could switch on the light without causing a fire. She would bet any sort of money that there wasn't even a fuse box.

She started to wonder what she had been thinking to not only accept this inheritance but to even move into this house. Presumably nothing or at least not terribly much. This was fast becoming a bit of a habit. She shook her head to herself. Sometimes she acted as naively and carelessly as a teenager and was then surprised when she stumbled from one catastrophe to the next but that was just the way she was. Chaos was her middle name.

In daylight, that bedside lamp was even uglier than at night, if that was possible. It would definitely have to go. It looked like the dust of decades had accumulated on the lampshade. Her great-aunt had certainly not been very house proud.

Julie reached out for the switch and pressed it. The bulb lit immediately. Hmm, so there was no power cut and the bulb was on. She had probably switched off the lamp last night and just didn't remember it.

By the time she had moved the heavy set of drawers away from the door, she had cursed herself multiple times and felt silly and ridiculous when thinking about her behaviour the night before. There had probably not been anyone on the attic. Perhaps a resident wild animal at most, whose noises had sounded unnaturally loud in the nightly silence. Or maybe she had just been dreaming.

As she now examined the dusty steps leading to the attic, at any rate, all she saw were her own footprints. Had there been another person, their soles must have had exactly the same size, shape and pattern as her own and they must have stepped directly into her own footprints. That did seem a bit unlikely.

The attic might, however, have a window through which the intruder may have come in and out, using a ladder. She needed to know. She climbed the stairs determinedly for the second time within in a few hours. Although the power was still on, she would have to come back with a torch to be able to see anything up there. The only thing she could say was that there was no window. The logical conclusion was that she had been alone in the house with Siyah all night and had only imagined the noises from the attic. She had always had a vivid imagination and it obviously ran away with her in this old, unfamiliar house.

»Good grief, Julie! Get a grip!« she scolded herself, switched off the light, turned around, closed the door behind her and went downstairs to the ground floor. She needed a cup of strong tea and a good breakfast. Fortunately, she had filled the larder yesterday. The nearest shop was quite a drive away and she was not keen on venturing there on a daily basis unless absolutely necessary. For the next few days, at least, she was well-stocked with a large variety of food.

And with cat food, of course. Siyah was already sitting in front of her bowl, impatient, and welcomed her with a reproachful meow.

»Good morning, Siyah.« Julie greeted her cat while hurrying to serve the requested food. »I'm sorry you had to wait so long for your breakfast, darling. I had an awful night. How about you? Where have you been? Did you sleep down here? You didn't see any burglars around the house by any chance, did you?« she kept talking to the cat. Too bad Siyah couldn't reply.

After brewing a large cup of strong tea with three spoons of sugar, she took milk, eggs and bacon from the fridge but grimaced in disgust when opening the bottle of milk she had bought the day before. It had definitely gone off. How had that happened? It had been fresh and kept chilled. Maybe the lid hadn't closed properly. How annoying! She would have to go food shopping again today after all, at least if she wanted milk in her next cup of tea.

»Can do without.« she shrugged and took a large sip of hot tea. She felt better in an instance. After a good helping of eggs and bacon with a large slice of fresh bread she would be ready for the day.

Julie opened the cupboard in which she had stowed her pots and pans and took out the one she needed. She dropped it with an appalled squeak and was lucky it missed her little toe by a mere inch. A broken toe was the last thing she needed. There was a dead mouse in the pan. Or there rather had been a dead mouse in the pan. It was now lying on the floor, next to the pan.

»Disgusting!« Julie shivered. If there was one thing she hated, then it was mice or rats. How many of them might live in this old house? Another thing she hadn't considered. And another item on her shopping list: mousetraps.

How had the dead mouse gotten into the pan? Jumped in alive, then died of a sudden heart attack? Weird. She really hoped this wasn't going to be a regular thing.

»Make sure you die outside next time!« was her strict instruction to any other mice and rats that might be in the house.

Siyah, who had meanwhile polished off her breakfast, came over, curious to see why her human was making such a fuss. »Good kitty. Take it away!« Julie pointed at the dead mouse, absurdly hoping the cat would take the mouse in her mouth, take it out of the house and drop it somewhere outside. Preferably without eating it. However, Siyah didn't think so. She just sniffed the mouse for a second, gave a sideward jerk and ran out of the room.

»You're round the bend, too.« Julie asserted dispassionately before starting her search for a brush and dustpan to get rid of the dead rodent. The dirty pan went into the bin, as well. Julie was pleased that after thorough inspection all other pots and pans had proven rodent-free and half an hour later she leaned back in the kitchen chair quite full. Now she needed a hot shower before she would make a start on her to-do list.

When Julie pressed the yellowed plastic switch, it took a little while for the artificial light to illuminate the small, windowless bathroom. Julie cast a probing look to the ceiling and frowned, unimpressed. A single ugly fluorescent lamp. That had to go, too, even before the bedside lamp and directly following the mattress. These fluorescent lamps tended to flicker, which triggered Julie's migraine attacks. Yet another item on her shopping list. About time she started actually writing that list down. It was getting difficult to remember everything.

She could only hope that this lamp was moisture-proof. After all, this bathroom had neither a window nor ventilation. When the house had been built at the beginning of the 20th century, nobody had spared a thought about that kind of thing and in later days no more had been modernised than what had been absolutely necessary.

Maybe the other bathrooms were better. Of course a house like this had not only the one bathroom but several. Today, Julie had chosen this particular bathroom as it was the only one with a shower. Then there was the larger main bathroom with the big cast-iron bathtub standing on lion's feet, which Julie was keen to check out at the next opportunity, as well as a tiny half bath with just a toilet and sink.

Julie opened the tap in the shower and tried to adjust the water to a reasonable temperature. Naturally, there was no mixer tap but two separate taps for hot and cold water. At first the water was freezing and of reddish colour. Julie sighed. The pipes were probably rusty. Hopefully they wouldn't burst. She really didn't need that. It would cost her a fortune to have all pipes in the house replaced. She wanted to put that off as long as possible. Moreover, she was not even sure to what extent renovation works were possible without major upheaval. She seemed to remember that the lawyer had said something about a »preservation order« during the execution of her great-aunts will but she had once again not paid attention as it had taken forever for the will to be read out loud and it had been so boring it made her yawn. She only understood half of the twisted sentences phrased in finest legalese anyway.

Needless to say, the bathroom didn't have any heating either so Julie hurried to get out of her dressing gown and pyjamas and under the hot shower as quickly as possible. But she stopped midway because she felt like she was being watched. Of course that was completely ridiculous as she was alone in the house with Siyah and the cat had definitely not followed her to the bathroom.

She thought she saw a movement in the mirror and turned around quickly so that she looked straight into it. She could see nothing but her own reflection but felt like she had just seen a flowing wisp of brown hair in the lower right corner of the mirror for a split second before it had disappeared. Julie laughed at herself. She definitely had a vivid imagination. If there had been any wisp of hair in the mirror at all, then it had been her own. Naturally her hair had flown given how quickly she had turned.

Still smiling, Julie got under the shower and drew the shower curtain. Another thing that would have to go. She hated that these things always came »cuddling« as she called it. Every time you were enjoying a nice hot shower, they were sucked inwards and clung to your body. Apparently, that had something to do with the hot steam but physics had never been her forte. In fact, she didn't care why they did it. She just found it yucky. Even more so with such an aged rag. She would definitely have a shower cubicle with a door installed.

Julie closed her eyes, lathered her hair and pleasurably let the hot water cascade over her – until she made a knee-jerk jump to the side, accompanied by a loud scream. From one second to the next the water had turned piping hot. Unless she wanted to regularly scald herself under the shower, she would have to get a modern mixer tap. Her arm, which the hot water had hit first, was bright red. She carefully reached out and tried to regulate the water temperature without scalding herself again but all of a sudden the water was now ice-cold.

»Bloody thing!« Julie grumbled angrily. Although she finally managed to adjust the water to the right temperate, the relaxing effect had waned, so she just quickly washed off the shampoo and shower gel before she got out. She wrung out her long wet hair, wrapping a towel around her head like a turban, rubbed herself dry and slipped into her fluffy dressing gown again.

When her eyes wandered over the mirror above the washbasin again by chance, she froze. It had steamed up but the word *OUT* was written over its full width in capital letters. It had clearly been written with a finger – but by whom? Actually, she was still sure there was no other person in the house and apart from that she would certainly have noticed if someone had sneaked in and out of the bathroom while she was showering, wouldn't she? Besides, she couldn't think of anyone who would want her out of the house. Who in their right senses would want this decrepit ruin anyway? Apart from herself, obviously.

The word had probably been there before and only become visible again now as the mirror had steamed up. Apparently, someone had played a trick at someone else's expense at some point and not only scared their original victim but Julie as well. Big time. For a second, her blood had curdled in her veins. Some people really had a strange sense of humour.

She picked up the bath towel she had carelessly dropped on the floor and used it to strenuously wipe the mirror. In the very same moment the fluorescent tube on the ceiling began to flicker with a sizzling noise before it went out entirely. Julie swore again: »For God's sake!« Properly bugged by now, she felt around for the door frame in the dark, groping for the light switch. When she pressed it, the light came on again. She urgently needed an electrician. And probably a plumber. As well as an architect, a structural engineer, a painter, a tiler, a carpenter, a slater, … Oh, bugger! Why the hell had she not simply stayed in her small city apartment? Could she still reject the inheritance now? Hardly. After all, she had already signed all the papers and even moved in.

»Sod it!«

She turned towards the mirror again and flinched, frightened.

As was to be expected, her reflection looked back at her – only that it wasn't her reflection. Although it looked exactly like her, its mouth had distorted to a crooked grin while she herself – and she was absolutely sure about that – was staring at the mirror with her mouth wide open in disbelief. She couldn't grasp what she was seeing. Then the grin in the mirror disappeared, her reflection squinted upwards and blew away a strand of hair that had fallen into its face. *Oh my God!* That was clearly not her reflection. Her wet hair was wrapped in a towel, after all, while the face in the mirror - which apart from this minor fact really was her spitting image - was framed by long, dry, curly strands falling openly over its shoulders.

Julie screamed. She screamed with all her might. And the face in the mirror started laughing hysterically. A loud, nasty, piercingly shrill laugh that made Julie shiver. And it didn't stop. On the contrary, it got louder and louder, so loud that Julie had to press her hands to her ears. Or was it her own scream that was ringing in her ears? After all, a reflection couldn't scream, or could it? Julie didn't care. She had to get out of here. She scrambled to the door in panic, threw it open and bolted towards her bedroom where she locked herself in again. As she was sprinting down the floor she heard the laughter stop and the same voice shout »OUT!« after her instead.

It took her a while to compose herself enough to get dressed but eventually she got into her car and drove to the small grocery in the village to buy fresh milk and maybe a bottle of booze which she would probably need to calm her nerves if things continued like this. The old house really seemed to fire her imagination. As far as the incident with her reflection in the mirror was concerned, however, she didn't have any doubts that she had not seen herself in the mirror, even though she couldn't logically explain it.

»You're not from here.« said the woman behind the counter with an unfriendly undertone and it was a statement, not a question. Julie was looked over from head to toe with blatant scepticism. She tried not to be irritated and gave the lady a friendly smile. »No, I've only been here since yesterday. My deceased great-aunt bequeathed the old manor to me and I moved in yesterday.« she explained. The elderly lady furrowed her brow.

»Maenor Tywyll?« she guessed. »Old Grace's rattrap? Well, you'll need to invest a fair bit of money in that to make it comfortable. Nothing has been modernised there for years.«

Julie was a bit miffed about the woman's inappropriate directness but tried to remain polite. »Yes, I have actually noticed that in the last twenty-four hours already.«

The woman seemed to suddenly realise that she had not been asked for her opinion. She smiled a placable smile and waved her hand dismissively.

»Oh well. Nothing that couldn't be fixed with a bit of commitment, a cleaning cloth and some good tools, right?«

Julie didn't reply. Her thoughts were already one step ahead. »Please tell me, do you know anyone who could have a look at my roof? I think it might have a few holes and leaks. I heard strange noises coming from the attic last night. Probably a marten or something like that. I would like to avoid a repeat performance if possible.«, Julie jabbered away nonchalantly and faked a happy smile. »That marten must weigh at least 200 pounds and wear army boots, judging by the way he tramped around up there.«

But the lady didn't laugh. On the contrary. She gave her an odd look and frowned as she quietly mumbled: »That's strange.«

»What is?« Julie asked, not smiling anymore either.

The woman, supposedly being the shopkeeper, hesitated for a moment before she replied: »Well, nothing really. It's just…old Gracie often said she heard someone walking around in the attic at night. We always laughed about it. She was quite old and a bit touched in the head, or at least that's what we thought. But now that you are saying the same…that really is a bit odd indeed. You'd better get an alarm system. Maybe some tramp has settled in your attic. You never know…«

»I…yes…erm…sure, thanks for the advice. I'll do that.« Julie stammered while her mind was reeling. Her great-aunt had heard those steps, too? So she hadn't imagined them. On the one hand, that was reassuring. On the other hand, it disturbed her even more. If the steps were real, then there had to be someone or something making them. She wanted neither tramps nor wildlife in her attic. She would definitely get a local specialist to examine her attic and seal the roof. She was in a sudden rush to pay and hurried out of the shop.

Julie parked her rattly and rusty Mini, which had definitely seen better times, in the drive to the old manor. Carrying her shopping up the three stone steps leading to the large wooden entrance door, she was surprised to find it gaping wide open. She hadn't locked it as she knew she wouldn't be long – and because there was nothing worth stealing anyway – but she had definitely closed it. Maybe the closing mechanism was broken. She would add a locksmith to the list of craftsmen she needed to contact.

Just as she was going to step inside, the heavy door slammed shut with a loud bang. Julie managed to jump backwards just in time, otherwise she would've had a broken foot now. She kicked the splintered wood that desperately needed a new coat of paint but surprisingly the door didn't swing open. Great, so the lock had finally snapped. A bit late. Julie put down her bags, fumbled for the keys and unlocked the door. At least that worked smoothly. She had almost expected the lock to jam and the key to break off.

She brought her shopping into the kitchen and was astonished to find the light on. Had she left it on in the morning? Obviously. Hearing a minatory growl behind her, she looked over her shoulder to see Siyah cowering in the corner, in fighting position, her eyes fixed on the larder which Julie had just been about to stock up with her shopping.

»What is it, silly? There's nothing there?« she asked her cat and opened the larder. Hissing loudly, Siyah jumped and bolted out of the kitchen as if Old Harry was after her. Julie shook her head. Apparently, this house didn't only afflict her but her cat, too. She called herself crazy when she realised she was relieved about having put away her shopping without finding any more dead rodents or anything eerie happening.

»At least the doorbell works.« Julie thought as it rang and made her jump. She hurried to the door where she was greeted by a good looking young man wearing a baseball cap.

»Oh, hello!« she said, surprised. She had not been expecting any visitors and never seen that man before.

»Hi! I'm Barry. I was at Maggie's shop and she told me to come over and have a look at your roof.« he said, introducing himself.

»Oh.« Julie repeated foolishly. Had the cat caught her tongue? Barry wasn't *that* good-looking. Or actually...tall, broad-shouldered, dark hair, bright blue eyes…he wasn't ugly. »Erm, yes. That's great! Come in. I'm Julie.« she found her words again. Together they climbed the stairs to the attic. Luckily, Barry had brought a powerful torch which perfectly illuminated even the furthest corner. He thoroughly checked the wooden beams and roof tiles and said it wouldn't do any harm to get the roof insulated. Julie pretended she hadn't heard that. She didn't need any more unexpected bills. Two hours later, Barry had indeed found a hole through which an animal could easily get in and out and had expertly sealed it.

»Alright« he said, stood up and wiped his dusty hands on his dungarees. »That's it. It should be quiet up here from now on.« He smiled contentedly.

»Fantastic!« Julie returned the smile. »Hopefully that means I can rest easy tonight.

The lady in the shop, I think you called her Maggie?, had suggested a tramp might live in my attic. I must admit I found the thought a bit unsettling. I'm glad it was just an animal after all.«

»A tramp wouldn't have been all that bad if he were friendly and only looking for somewhere to sleep. As long as it's not that lunatic…!«

»What lunatic?« Julie asked, alarmed.

»Haven't you heard?« Barry was surprised. »It's been on the news for days. A patient has gone missing from a psychiatric clinic and disappeared without a trace. They're looking for him all over the country but to no avail so far. You'd better lock all doors and windows when you're all alone in this big old house.«

Julie felt a bit uncomfortable. »I'll do that for sure.«

»Great. I'd better get going before my other customers complain about me taking so long.«

»Erm, sure. Of course. What do I owe you?«

»I'll pop round with the invoice over the next few days, okay?« Barry suggested.

»Okay.«

Once the handsome tradesman had left, Julie scoffed a cheese sandwich and a cup of tea for lunch and decided to have a look around the in-house library, choose a good book and spend the afternoon reading. She had more than enough to do but simply didn't feel like it today. Tomorrow was another day.

Julie's eyes lit up as soon as she entered the library. She loved books and she loved that dry, slightly dusty smell of old paper. This library was heaven. It alone had made it worth moving into this semi-ruined house. Three sides of the room were lined with countless shelves, each one ceiling-high. There was a wooden ladder which enabled you to reach even the topmost compartments. In between the shelves, there were several small tables, each equipped with a chair and a reading lamp. They had probably once served as desks. The fourth wall was dominated by a big fireplace. In front of it, a huge, pretty ugly, worn wing chair made of pea-green velvet and a small, round ebony coffee table had been arranged on an old, faded Persian carpet that wasn't any nicer than the rest of the furniture. The ensemble was completed by a matching drinks trolley on which Julie spotted a formidable assortment of gin, whisky, brandy and port. She could have saved the money for the booze this morning.

Once again Julie let her eyes wander across the room. It was perfect! As ugly, old-fashioned and outworn as the individual furnishings were, they perfectly matched each other, the room and its atmosphere. She walked along surveying the shelves, each neatly labelled with metal plates, and finally stopped in front of the one holding local tales and myths. Since there were a good few of those in Wales, the shelf held countless books on the topic. Awestruck, Julie carefully touched the ancient, brittle leather spines of the books until suddenly one of them slipped off the shelf and fell to the floor. She picked it up and threw a glance at the title. *The Gwyllion*. She hadn't the faintest idea who or what the Gwyllion was or were but she immediately noticed the great similarity to the name of the village: Gwyllin.

»Why not?« she asked herself. Myths and tales could be very entertaining and maybe she would learn something about the local history from it. She took the book but decided against the scuffed wing chair and headed instead for the antiquated chaise longue standing in front of the window in one of the rooms on the ground floor which she had discovered the day before. She assumed that it had once been the parlour in which the lady of the house had received her friends for afternoon tea. There was a bell with a string on the wall which may have been used to ring for the maid to demand tea and biscuits. Unfortunately, Julie had to get her own tea and biscuits but at least Siyah made an appearance and curled up on her lap once she had made herself comfortable on the chaise longue with the ponderous tome. The fan heater in the corner worked just fine and kept the room toasty, although Julie didn't even want to think about how much electricity it used. She opened the weighty screed and was captivated as soon as she started reading the first page.

Gwyllion or Gwyllon are Welsh ghosts or night-wanderers up to no good. According to folklorists, they are female fairies of frightful aspect, gloomy spirits more akin to hags or witches. They haunt abandoned valleys and lonely roads in the Welsh mountains, waiting for their unsuspecting victims. Those who encounter them either by night or on a misty day are sure to lose their way even if they are perfectly familiar with the road. In most cases they are never to be seen again but horrible screams can be heard at the moment of their disappearance.

Few travellers were lucky enough to escape them so that they could report on their experience. One man reported meeting an old woman on a mountain road and at the same time found that he had lost his way. Thinking she was human he called out for her to stay but receiving no answer he thought she was deaf. He tried to overtake her but she led him further astray, always out of reach, until he found himself in a marsh. When she uttered a cackling laugh he suspected she might be a Gwyll. His grandmother had told him the old tales about the Gwyllion so he knew there was one thing they feared. A knife. It is well known that the Gwyllion are afraid of cold steel and can be banished by it.

Another traveller reported he had encountered several such female spirits at night on a pass where they danced fancifully around him. At the same time he heard the sounds of a fox horn and what seemed like invisible hunters riding by on their horses. Although afraid he drew his knife and immediately the fairies vanished.

Some particularly wily Gwyllion come into the houses of the people, especially in stormy weather when they seek shelter. When this happens one should under any circumstances make them welcome, not out of any sense of friendship but out of fear of what they might do to them if they were offended. They should be provided with clean water, hot broth and a slice of bread and care should be taken that no knife or any other cutting tool shall be in the corner near the fire where the fairies like to *sit. While it is desirable to exorcise them when in the open air, it is not prudent to display an inhospitable attitude towards any member of the fairy realm.*

Fascinated, Julie devoured the pages about the Gwyllion and wondered whether it was just coincidence or whether the village of Gwyllin had intentionally been named after those vicious spirits from Welsh mythology. After all, the two words differed by merely one letter. Would she be able to find out? And if it wasn't coincidence – which seemed likely as such coincidence would be almost too much -, what was the story behind it? Had the village frequently been haunted by night-wanderers? That would be a bit creepy. Being a modern woman, of course Julie was thinking rationally and was well aware that ghosts didn't really exist. She was, however, also Welsh and deep inside all Welsh believed in ghosts and fairies, at least a tiny little bit, even those who would never publicly admit it. Those myths and legends had deep roots in the Welsh culture.

A cool draught blew past her and Julie shivered. Not surprising, given the old, single-glazed windows. She would have to live with those a little while longer as she just couldn't afford to get all windows in the house replaced. A new burglar-proof front door had priority over that, too.

Julie heard a small noise to her right and turned to see what had caused it. She couldn't believe her eyes. She opened her mouth but was tongue-tied. The small black and white photo in the tarnished silver frame was moving as if by magic on the teapoy on which it had been placed. Bit by bit, more and more to the left, until it fell to the floor.

Julie jumped off the chaise longue and picked up the picture frame. Luckily, the thick carpet had absorbed the shock so that the glass had not broken. Julie put the photo neatly back on the teapoy but it immediately tipped over and fell on the glass. Julie began to tremble. Not only because of these eerie incidents but also because it was suddenly stone-cold in the room. Not just a bit chilly, no. Absolutely freezing cold like in an ice room. The cold crept into every fibre of her body, into her bones, up her spine, into her hair ends and finger tips. Never in her life had she been so cold.

She mustered all her courage and put the picture frame back up again. A mere second later it was lifted into the air by an invisible force and smashed against the wall with a loud bang. This time the glass shattered into a thousand pieces. Julie threw her hands up in front of her face to protect her eyes against the shards that were flying in all directions.

She carefully approached the picture frame and turned it but it was impossible to say what could once be seen in the old photo. Julie had seen it the day before. It was the photograph of two little girls, maybe five or six years old, straw-hatted and dressed in old-fashioned ruffle dresses. They were standing in front of a rose bush, holding hands and looking at the camera, uniformly stony-faced. Twins, like two peas in a pod.

But this was no longer visible in the picture. Instead there was a large, dispersed black colour stain, almost like an inkblot. Julie could no longer explain this as vivid imagination or bad dreams. She was wide awake and this had really just happened. Something was not right here.

»What's going on?« she whispered when suddenly the phone rang. The telephone that didn't even exist in the house.

Julie remained motionless for a moment, just listening to the phone bell. Could it be that there actually was a telephone line and even a telephone set in the house? Maybe she had simply overlooked it during her first stock-take? Admittedly, she had not been too thorough, she had just wanted to get a general idea of what was in the house.

She followed the sound of the phone bell out of the room, down the long hallway and round a corner into a side corridor she did not remember. There, in a dark corner, stood a double door wooden cupboard of the kind that had been used for storing linen and other household items in days gone by. The sound led her directly there.

Julie opened the doors of the cupboard which as almost empty. Its only contents were a big, black, old-fashioned telephone standing on one of the middle shelves – ringing. Julie was confused. She couldn't see any cable. She examined the phone from all sides, carefully lifting it, while it continued to ring unflinchingly. Indeed, it had no cable. But it rang.

She put it back into the cupboard and looked at it pensively. It made no sense at all. Should she pick up the receiver? Maybe not. She brought herself to do it, mainly because the constant ringing was very unnerving.

»Hello?«

Finally the ringing stopped. At first there was silence on the other end of the line, then she heard a whistling. The caller – the voice definitely sounded female – was whistling a song. A scary, doleful tune. It gave Julie the creeps.

»Who is this?« Julie demanded but did not receive a reply. The whistling stopped. Julie hung up, shaking her head, and immediately the strange tune set in again, only much louder now and in the direction Julie had come from. So she retraced her steps along the hallway and the whistling grew ever louder with each step until she found herself standing in the parlour again where she had been sitting on the chaise longue just a few minutes ago. The gramophone, which stood in one corner of the room and which Julie had admired the day before but had been unable to get working, was blaring the same tune on full volume. She switched it off and gave a sigh of relief when the noise stopped. She had a terrible headache now.

The relief was short lived, however. Loud clashing and clanking was coming from the kitchen. Julie gave an irritated groan. What now? On her way to the kitchen she passed the front door and noticed that the postman must meanwhile have been there. Several letters, leaflets and a newspaper had been delivered through the letter box. She stooped down to pick them up and realised that they were torn and in tatters.

»Siyah!« she called out furiously. How dare this cat? Why had she ripped up all the post? She had never done that before. The paper scraps in her hands, Julie headed for the kitchen where she gave a horrified yelp. The doors of all cupboards stood open and all her dishes lay on the floor, broken. Not a single plate, mug or soup bowl was left in the cupboard. Everything was lying at her feet, shattered to pieces. To top it all, the water tap was open and as the drain was blocked with shards the sink was already overflowing and flooding the kitchen.

»Shit!« Julie shouted and carefully waded through the water and the shards towards the sink to close the tap. What was going on here?

This mess could definitely not have been caused by Siyah. The cat could open neither cupboards nor water taps. That was impossible. So maybe she hadn't ripped up the post either? By now Julie was convinced that this house was haunted.

She spent over an hour picking up broken dishes and mopping up water. Just as she was done, she heard Siyah growl loudly. The black cat was cowering in front of the larder, a few steps away from its door, had flattened her ears and bristled her fur. She seemed to feel very uneasy about something.

»What's wrong, Siyah?« Julie asked soothingly. »Is there a mouse in there?« She went to the larder to have a look but for every step she took towards it, Siyah backed off a little bit more, making minacious noises, without taking her eyes off the larder door. As

Julie flung the door open, Siyah gave a loud hiss and bolted pell-mell out of the room.

Everything was in perfect order in the larder. Julie couldn't find anything unusual. Siyah must have just imagined something.

After warming up a semi-tasty can of tomato soup and spooning it directly from the pot, she decided to go to bed and watch some TV.

When Julie entered her bedroom, it was freezing in there. The window was wide open and the terribly kitschy curtains were blowing in the wind.

»Stop it!« she hissed at the invisible ghost whom by now she blamed for all the inexplicable events. She wasn't even scared anymore, she was just fed up.

She closed the window, lit a fire in the fireplace, snuggled up in bed and switched on the old tube TV – one of the very few nearly modern comforts her great-aunt had indulged in. She watched a not particularly fascinating documentary about gerbils, switched the TV off early and fell asleep relatively quickly.

She woke up around 2 a.m., as a quick look at the alarm clock told her, because she was cold. Again the window was wide open, so she got up and closed it. As she was about to go back to bed she noticed that the bedroom door stood open, too. She was absolutely sure that she had closed it in the evening.

She closed it again, resolutely, and turned the key twice. Good, this door wasn't going to be opened again tonight. The fire had burnt down and wasn't giving off any heat anymore. She had walked to the window barefoot and the cold was creeping into her body through her bare feet now. She hurried back to bed and got under the blanket but just as she sat in bed she saw from the corner of her eye that the door stood open once again.

»What do you want from me, for heaven's sake?« she called out helplessly into the dark. It seemed almost like a response when the light went on in the bedroom, followed by the light in the corridor.

»You want me to leave the room?« The light flickered for a second which she interpreted as a Yes. She put on slippers and dressing gown and left the room. The stairs to the attic were lit as well and again she could hear footsteps from above. Not heavy and shuffling as in the first night but rather quick and staccato-like as if someone was running around in high heels.

When Julie reached the top step the attic door stood open, the lights were on and she heard a knocking. As soon as she had stepped inside, the door slammed shut behind her and the lights went off.

»Hey!« she shouted, wanting to open the door again but the doorknob didn't turn. The door was locked. And the light switch didn't work either. She started to panic now.

»Let me out right now!« she screamed but to no avail.

Instead the knocking got louder. It seemed to be coming from the opposite wall. Carefully, hoping not to stumble over anything in the dark, Julie found her way to the source of the noise by touching the walls. And indeed it was even louder there. It was knocking inside the wall, as if someone had been mured in there and was hammering against the wall from inside.

Julie didn't know what to do. She raised her hand and knocked at the wall lightly. She immediately received a respondent knock. She knocked twice and two knocks came back. Now she knocked three times, just to be absolutely sure, and received three knocks in response.

»Is…is there someone inside the wall?« she stammered, feeling quite silly. How would a living person have gotten inside the wall after all? On the other hand, anything seemed possible in this house.

The knocking stopped and was replaced by a scratching. It scratched and scraped inside the wall as if someone was trying to dig through the stone. Maybe just a mouse? But then she heard a voice.

»Out!« It sounded hushed, almost a whisper, but was repeated over and over again in regular short intervals, getting louder and clearer each time.

»Out! Out! Out! OUT! OUT!«

And then the knocking resumed, rather a hammering now. Someone seemed to be punching the wall with both hands from inside, yelling »Out!« non-stop.

First she had been told to come here and now she was told to go? Whoever that ghost was, he – or she – needed to make up their mind.

»Alright, I'm leaving!« she yelled at the ghost, searching for the door which she was luckily able to open again now. She ran down the stairs and through the corridor back to her bedroom. This time the window was closed but the glass now had a huge crack across its full length.

The next morning Julie felt pretty exhausted. She had lain wide awake for the rest of the night and racked her brain about the knocking and the voice inside the wall. Could it be that someone really had been mured alive in there? Rubbish, of course not. She had seen the walls when she had been up there with Barry. The wall plaster was really old. If someone had been mured in the attic at all then it had happened ages ago and that person was long since dead and had dissolved into dust.

After brewing herself some strong coffee and drinking it from a juice glass – she didn't have any mugs left after all -, Julie drove to the village again to purchase new dishes, cups, mugs and bowls at the small household supply shop as well as a small fan heater, an electric torch and batteries, a couple of doorstops and a few mousetraps – just in case. She couldn't resist getting some soul food as well - a bag of crisps and a ridiculous number of chocolate bars – before making another couple of stops at other shops.

On her way back she called in at various tradesmen, asking them to stop by the manor when they had a chance. She had no idea how she would pay their bills but some repairs just couldn't wait. Most importantly, her bedroom window needed new glass as soon as possible unless she wanted to freeze to death at night.

She also made a stopover at the local pub where she treated herself to some much needed fish and chips for lunch, together with a nice cold beer. There she overheard that »the lunatic«, as Barry had called him, had still not been found. The authorities had still not disclosed any details either. Nobody knew whether that person was male or female, which clinic they had escaped from nor why he or she had been treated there. The authorities only warned the public to exercise extreme caution and asked that anything unusual be reported to the police.

Julie could have informed the police about all sorts of unusual observations but doubted that they would take her seriously and certainly didn't want to risk taking the absconder's place in the psychiatric clinic herself. Surely the police had no time for ghost stories and night-time spectres. She didn't blame them.

She spent the afternoon sanding the wooden front door, then giving it a new coat with the bright red paint she had bought in the village. Not that it made the door any more stable or burglar-proof but at least it looked nicer and until she was able to afford a new front door this was the best she could do.

Just before nightfall she also managed to plant the two rose bushes she had not been able to resist buying at the local market garden in the flower tubs next to the front door.

All day long she felt a strange inner tension and was expecting something paranormal to happen at any moment but it didn't. It was just an ordinary day and there was nothing even faintly unusual about it. Absolute bliss! Maybe the ghost had vanished? She didn't really dare to believe it yet but her mood was definitely improving.

Everything remained quiet in the evening as well and exhausted from her busy day, Julie fell asleep on the threadbare flowery settee in the living room. Although she did wake up in the middle of the night again, this time it was just because her back hurt. She went upstairs, went to bed and slept like a log for the rest of the night.

When she woke up the next morning, she felt very well-rested and was in the best mood she had been in for a long time. She was bursting with energy and spent all day clearing out the miscellaneous cabinets in the house, cramming the bins with all sorts of junk.

Carrying a pile of moth-eaten tablecloths outside, she was shocked to find herself humming the creepy tune which the ghost had whistled over the phone. Oh dear, things had become pretty bad! She quickly trawled her not very extensive memory bank for a different song and began singing a pretty out-of-tune version of Green Day's *Basket Case*.

»Oh, well done, Julie. Fantastic choice!« she said to herself, her voice full of sarcasm, and shook her head, half amused, half irritated. Why had she remembered this particular song?

After all, *Basket Case* was a slang term for a person with serious mental problems or with generally little or no hope. She seemed to remember having read somewhere that Billie Joe Armstrong, the band's lead singer and guitarist, had written this song to cope with his anxiety, panic attacks and emotional instability. From this point of view, maybe the song had been the obvious choice. She was either going absolutely paranoid in this house or at least developing hallucinations. She was definitely not stoned, and although she could rule out this option from the lyrics, it would have been the most reassuring alternative.

Given that more than 24 hours had passed without any worrying events, Julie could only laugh to herself. There was most likely a rational explanation for all of this, optical and acoustical illusions or something like that. Maybe she should have paid more attention in her physics lessons at school.

»Ouch!« she squealed when she suddenly fell and hit her head on the edge of the doorstep. She stood up and rubbed the aching spot on her temple. That was going to be a big bump. Someone had pushed her. She hadn't tripped, she had been pushed. Had she counted her chickens before they had hatched? Was the ghost still there?

»I need a cuppa.« she decided and headed to the kitchen to put the kettle on. She switched on the antiquated radio set and heard the presenter talk about share prices. »I don't care.« Julie said and changed to a different frequency. Unfortunately, however, she didn't seem to receive any other programme over the radio, no matter which one she tried. All she could hear was a static. »Alright, share prices then.« she gave in and changed back to the original frequency where the presenter had meanwhile finished his report. Now she could hear a piano playing a tune she recognised right away. The ghost's tune. She quickly switched off the radio. She may not have been all that wrong about hallucinating.

Although she wasn't really hungry, she put two slices of toast in the toaster and took butter and strawberry jam from the fridge just to distract herself. Maybe she had only imagined the piano playing because her blood sugar was low.

What was that sudden burning smell? Julie turned, looking around, and immediately noticed the blaze coming out of the toaster. She frantically scanned the kitchen for something she could use to extinguish the flames and grabbed a bottle of coke that caught her eye. Luckily, it was easy enough to put out the small fire.

»Very nice, coke flavoured toast!« Julie joked although she wasn't in a laughing mood. If that ghost was now moving on to setting things on fire, her problem was much bigger than she had thought. She had better come up with a good solution but what could that be? Glass-moving games, scrying and card reading were out of the question. Ouija Boards even more so.

She had a creepy feeling about those. What then? She couldn't think of anything off the top of her head.

The sun had set by now. After feeding Siyah, Julie nestled up on the settee with a cup of tea and a crossword. Siyah was lazily lying next to her, grooming her belly, when the big standard lamp, which stood directly next to the settee and was their only source of light, began to buzz and flicker.

»Oh no, here we go again! Please don't!« Julie whinged.

The cat was clearly finding the situation a bit fishy, too. She had jumped off the settee as if stung by an adder, warily closed in on the standard lamp and was now remaining motionless in a defensive position. She had arched her back, bristled her fur, flattened her ears and was giving threating hisses. Again the bulb in the standard lamp flickered, the buzzing increased and Siyah hissed even more loudly. Fear crept into her body and mind as Julie stood still and watched the events. Eventually, the bulb burnt out with a quiet but clearly audible *CLICK* and the living room lay in complete darkness. However, not in complete silence. A high voice started whistling the tune of the ghost. Siyah hissed once again, then Julie felt the cat's tail touch her leg as the feline raced out of the room.

Even more frightened now, Julie carefully moved towards the fireplace where several candles and a box of matches had been placed. Either her great-aunt had had a romantic streak and enjoyed candlelit evenings or – and this seemed a lot more likely to Julie – power cuts were a regular occurrence here, for all other rooms were equipped with candles and matches as well.

When she finally felt the matchbox under her fingers, she lit a match and then a candle with it. One by one she lit all the candles on the mantelpiece, then looked around warily. As soon as she had lit the first candle the whistling had stopped. Julie gave a sigh of relief. That tune really scared her although she couldn't say why, but she had rejoiced too soon. A cold draught came up and within a second all candle flames died. At the same time, the whistling set in again, louder and more haunting now. And more intense. It almost felt like it was inside Julie's head.

»No! No, no, no, no, no!« she screamed and pressed both hands against her ears. But it didn't help, the tune only got louder. Now panicking, Julie began to shake her head as if she could shake off the eldritch tune. But to no avail. The whistling grew ever louder and caused her a splitting headache. Julie lost her nerve.

»Stop it, for fuck's sake!« she raged, and really…the tune stopped.

Very slowly she took her hands off her ears and lowered her arms. She was expecting to hear the whistling again immediately but fortunately did not. Julie was standing in the dark, listening hard. Nothing.

»What is it that you want from me?« she whispered into the silence.

The bulb in the old standard lamp flickered once in response, only to die away again.

»What do you want?« Julie repeated and again the bulb flared up for one moment.

Julie couldn't see in the darkness but heard a scratching noise as if someone was hastily scribbling something on a piece of paper with a pencil. Then the light came on again and this time it remained on. From the corner of her eye

Julie saw something move on the coffee table and heard a low clattering. She looked closer and saw the pen she had used to fill in the crossword roll around on the table. A single word was written all over the page in spidery handwriting: *OUT!*

»Why do you want to get rid of me?"« Julie asked cautiously. The light flared up again.

»What do you have against me?"« The light stayed off.

»Why do you want me to leave?« The light remained off. Okay, that was obviously the wrong question.

»Are you real?« she asked the question which seemed pretty stupid to her but which was preying on her mind.

The light went on and Julie shuddered.

»Who are you?«

Immediately, the pen started dashing over the crossword again. Again just one word, again just four letters. As it was written across the previous word, it took Julie a moment to spot it.

AMIE

»Your name is Amie?« she asked and the light jittered.

»Okay.« Julie said, trying to stay calm even though her panic was surging again. »Hello Amie.«

Again the light flashed.

»Do you need my help?« Julie asked with bated breath. Another flash of light.

»Erm, okay. How can I help you?«

So fast that she hardly noticed it, an invisible hand ripped the curtains off the curtain rail and knocked over the standard lamp so that Julie was standing in the dark again. A split second later a direful scream resounded at a deafening volume and curdled Julie's blood.

»*OUT!*«

And Julie ran. She ran as if the devil were after her. She ran out of the room, tripped over the carpet in the hallway and fell, grazed her knee, struggled to her feet again and kept running. Up the stairs, into her bedroom where she locked the door and blocked it with the heavy old chest of drawers again. This was, of course, unnecessary. If Amie was indeed real and indeed a ghost, it was very unlikely that she would enter the room through the door. Nonetheless, the barricaded door made Julie feel slightly safer.

She leaned against the wall, closed her eyes and concentrated on breathing calmly and regularly until her pulse slowed down and she had pulled herself together a little bit. Only then did she slowly open her eyes again. At this very moment the bedside lamp was switched on and Julie cracked up.

»No! Stop it! Fuck off! Leave me alone!« she screamed and began to cry hysterically. As a result, the bedside lamp was thrown across the room and crashed into the mirror on the dressing table, causing it to break into a myriad of pieces with a loud clink, accompanied by furious screams of »*OUT!*«

»Fuck off!« Julie screeched once again, ran over to the bed, hid under the blanket and cried hysterically into her pillow. She was so scared.

What should she do?

It took Julie a long time to get a grip on herself. Her entire body was shivering and it was only due to sheer exhaustion that she finally fell into a restless sleep. She kept jolting awake from dreadful nightmares in which she was hunted by a ghost in a mirror who drove her to death.

In the middle of the night she heard a scratching noise at the door and panicked again in an instant.

»Go away!« she shouted but the scratching didn't stop. On the contrary, it got louder and more determined.

»Go away!«

»*MEOW!*« came a heartbreaking cry from the other side of the door.

»Oh my goodness, Siyah! My poor baby!« Julie called out, terrified. She jumped out of bed and hurried to push the set of drawers away from the door so that she could let the cat in. Siyah came dashing in as soon as the door was opened. Julie quickly picked her up and buried her face in the cat's fluffy black fur.

»I'm sorry, darling. I'm so sorry!« she reaffirmed and covered the cat's head in countless kisses.

She spent the rest of the night sitting in bed upright and tense, the cat on her lap, giving her the comfort she needed so desperately. Her life had turned into a nightmare since she had moved into this house. If only she had stayed in Cardiff!

What if she simply moved out again? Would she get rid of Amie this way? Could you shake off a ghost so easily? Or would Amie follow her wherever she went? She made a mental note to check the book about the Gwyllion again for the part where it explained how to get rid of night-wanderers. But of course she didn't know whether Amie was a Gwyll at all or a different kind of spirit. Or did she only exist in her imagination? She simply didn't know but if there was a way to get rid of her she had to find it because one thing she knew for sure: If it continued like this, she would definitely lose her mind.

She couldn't help thinking of the film *The Exorcist* but of course that was nonsense. First of all, the plot of that film was pure fiction while Amie seemed very real to her. Secondly, she could hardly approach the local priest with a story about a face in a mirror and a creepy tune in a cable-less telephone and hire him for an exorcism just like that. She highly doubted that in this day and age priests still made house calls during which they carried a crucifix in front of them and splashed holy water just because someone had told them something about an alleged ghost. More likely, he would think she was off her rocker and she would end up in a psychiatric clinic, wearing a straightjacket.

Her thoughts were going round in circles. She wasn't able to think straight and was glad when dawn finally set in.

Everything was quiet the entire next day but by now Julie had developed such a constant underlying tension that she was in alarm mode non-stop and couldn't relax at all anymore. She only left the bed to feed Siyah and to get food and drink for herself or to use the toilet. She didn't even dare take a shower.

After having been awake all night, of course she was completely worn out now but too scared to go to sleep. To make things worse, she had a searing headache again which she tried to fight with lashings of painkillers, but to no avail. Every time she did fall asleep for a short while, she was plagued by nightmares again.

The following two days passed in a similar way. Sleepless nights and restless days full of fear and vague apprehension. And constant headaches. She wasn't hungry at all, however. All this madness seemed to have spoilt her appetite. She only left her bedroom when absolutely necessary. She left the house just once after four days and only very quickly to stock up on Siyah's cat food. The doorbell rang once or twice but she ignored it. She was in no state to open the door to anyone. She felt unable to discuss repairs with tradesmen, however urgent they might be.

After her short shopping trip, Julie felt completely exhausted and retreated to her bedroom again. Strangely enough, she didn't feel protected there but still somewhat safe although strange things had happened in this room as well.

She spent several hours scanning the newspaper for property adverts as she had realised that she would go crazy if she stayed in this house permanently. She had to get out of here and back to Cardiff as soon as possible. Back to a small flat in the city where life was buzzing around her rather than sitting in a huge old house all by herself and being terrorised by a ghost called Amie who clearly wanted to get rid of her. Julie would have loved to do Amie that favour but unfortunately she quickly realised that the she couldn't afford any of the vacant flats. Not even a tiny room in a shared flat. Rental prices had surged again and since she hadn't been working for a while her financial situation wasn't exactly rosy. Even less so being a freelancer with no regular income. Not exactly what landlords preferred.

Maybe she could stay with a friend or workmate for a while? She hadn't brought herself to ask one yet. It could only be a temporary solution in any case, nothing permanent. First of all she needed a long-term perspective but that was a distant prospect. For the time being she had no other choice but to stay in Amie's house unless she wanted to become homeless, and given the Welsh weather she wasn't particularly keen on that.

Amie's house. That was what she called this house now. She had been naïve to think it was her house. It was not and never had been. Even before she had first arrived, this house had been occupied. By Amie. And Amie was obviously not willing to give it up without a fight nor to share it with Julie.

Julie had brought the old book about the Gwyllion to her bedroom as she wanted to search it again for any hints about how to get rid of a Gwyll. If she could find anything on that in the book, she would give it a try. Just one. If it went wrong, Julie had better disappear into thin air. You didn't mess with ghosts and definitely not with Amie.

Unfortunately, she still had no idea whether Amie was a Gwyll or some other kind of spirit. What kinds of spirits were there anyway?

Poltergeists, of course. But apart from those? She didn't have the foggiest notion.

Several hours passed as Julie went through the book looking for indications and took notes of everything that may come in handy. However, as the book concentrated exclusively on the Gwyllion, she would have to get another book about ghosts in general – and especially about ways to get rid of them. The library probably held extensive literature on this topic.

She was so concentrated on her research that she was totally tuned out to her surroundings. When she finally did look up, she noticed a slow movement from the corner of her eye. The double door of the built-in wardrobe opened as if by an invisible hand. No, not *as if*. It did open by an invisible hand. Amie obviously needed attention again.

She could simply have ignored it, of course, but she had always had a compulsive sense of order and had never liked open doors. Her zodiac sign was Virgo, after all. So she got up and closed the wardrobe door but as soon as she returned to the bed it stood open again. This scene repeated itself several times until Julie had had enough. She dug out an old pair of tights from her great-aunt's chest of drawers and knotted it around the wardrobe handles so that they couldn't open anymore. Julie grinned, pleased with herself.

Amie, however, was not happy at all about this interference. A framed picture came flying off the wall.

»Whatever…« Julie said, shrugging, and ignored the other two pictures that fell off the wall, too, one by one. She had never liked them anyway, so Amie was welcome to break them.

A look through the window told her that it was pitch-dark by now. She had lost all sense of time during the past few days which had been mostly spent behind locked doors. She had given up any daily routine.

Her head was spinning from all the reading, her eyes were overstrained and her legs had gone to sleep after sitting cross-legged for quite a while, tingling uncomfortably. Julie yawned, put the heavy book aside and stood up to stretch. She decided to watch some TV and chose a travel documentary. Once that was over, she switched off the light and slept like a baby for the first time in days. Either that was due to sleep deprivation or it was true that you eventually got used to everything. Even ghosts.

Piercing screams woke her. Julie jolted awake and looked around, alarmed. The screams were coming from the television. The television she had turned off hours ago. She was absolutely sure about that. Now it was on again and not even showing the program she had watched last. There had been a theme night and a commercial saying that there would be travel documentary after travel documentary all night long. But what was flickering across the screen right now was neither the same channel nor a travel documentary. She recognised the horror film right away. It was *The Ring,* namely the very scene in which the dead girl's ghost was coming out of the TV screen. Julie had always found that one particularly scary. Thankfully, nothing and nobody was coming out of her own TV screen but there was a different analogy to the film: The unconnected telephone on the ground floor was ringing. So loudly that she could hear it in her bedroom.

Julie froze and anxiously clawed the blanket. She was so scared, she couldn't even scream. One thing was for sure: No matter how long that phone might ring, she would never ever pick up. As soon as she had overcome her state of shock, she jumped out of bed and turned off the TV. Immediately, the phone stopped ringing, too. But why had there been screams anyway? Julie had watched the film several times and knew that nobody was screaming in that scene, definitely not a woman anyway. Every single hair on her body stood on end.

While Julie was still trying to comprehend the situation, someone knocked on the door. Once, twice, three times, four times. The knocking got louder and more insistent each time and finally sounded really angry. Julie did not stir. After a while, the knocking stopped and it was silent for one second until someone started rattling at the door aggressively.

Fortunately, she had blocked it with the heavy set of drawers again!

»Go away!« Julie shouted, her voice trembling with fear, and indeed the rattling stopped.

Only moments later, something white appeared in the small gap under the door, in the right corner, the only part that wasn't blocked by the chest of drawers. A piece of paper that was being slipped under the door. Slowly and as quietly as possible Julie tiptoed to the door, reached out for the note and picked it up. As she had expected, again there was just one single word scribbled on it: *OUT!*

She tore the note to pieces and threw the snippets into the fire which had a tiny glow left. Furious howling set in on the other side of the door, becoming louder and louder. Julie pressed both hands to her ears until it finally stopped. Then there was silence, at last. Had she beat Amie this round? She couldn't really believe it. The knot in her stomach grew bigger. She had a bad feeling about this. Once again she told herself that she really had to move out soon, before it was too late.

Hang on! *Before it was too late*? This thought was new and it horrified her. Thinking about it again, however, it matched her gut feeling. Something told her that this wasn't going to end well unless she gave up the house. Amie wasn't going to leave her alone and there wasn't going to be a compromise either. Only one of them could win this and Julie had a bad feeling that it wasn't going to be her. So she had better hurry up and find out if and how she could get rid of Amie.

At the crack of dawn, Julie gathered her courage and left the bedroom. She ordered pizza al tonno and a bottle of white wine – her first proper meal in days – and enjoyed them to the fullest. She wolfed down the pizza at record speed and it was only now that she realised how ravenous she really was. She quaffed the wine way too hastily so that she felt a bit tipsy. Or maybe that was because it was very early in the morning. She had obviously been lucky and found a 24/7 delivery service. Since she hadn't had any form of daily routine for quite some time now, she hadn't given any thought about whether pizza and wine made a good breakfast. She had just felt like it and placed her order without thinking about it twice.

However, her tipsiness didn't stop her from turning every single room in the house upside down. She was searching for clues about Amie but couldn't find anything. Not a single hint. No indication that a girl or woman called Amie had ever lived in this house.

She found more photos of the twins she had first seen on the picture in the parlour which Amie had thrown against the wall in anger. At least Julie assumed that it had been Amie. She really didn't want to imagine that there could be more than just one aggressive ghost here. One of that sort was more than enough already.

Some of the photos were labelled and told Julie that neither of the twin girls had been called Amie and after studying the family tree she knew that neither of them had met an early or unnatural death. Her assumption that Amie was the ghost of one of those twin girls didn't seem right but she didn't have any other idea. She twisted her mind for another theory she could rationalise but nothing seemed even remotely plausible to her. How frustrating! She pushed these thoughts aside and went to the library instead to look for books about ghosts in general and possible exorcisms in particular. As she had expected, she found quite a few, chose the one that looked most promising and took it to the scuffed wing chair.

She gathered from the book that there was a surprisingly large number of spirits. On the one hand there were friendly spirits like tutelary spirits, natural spirits, animal spirits and sky spirits. The first few chapters of the book were dedicated to them but Julie skipped them as Amie was clearly none of those sweet-tempered spirits.

Chapters about revenants, orbs, ghosts and other phantoms followed. None of them seemed to be very dangerous and they weren't described as being aggressive so Amie was probably none of them either.

The last part of the book was devoted to the far more distressing representatives of the beyond: incubi, poltergeists and demons.

Much to Julie's disappointment, their descriptions didn't really seem to match Amie either and she was probably not a Gwyll if the descriptions of that species were to be believed. It was like looking for a needle in a haystack. Not the best preconditions, Julie thought, because she suffered from full-blown hay fever. This silly thought made her giggle. At least she hadn't lost her sense of humour.

Out of the blue she remembered that she hadn't fed Siyah today. The poor thing was probably desperate for her breakfast. Taking two steps at a time, Julie hurried downstairs.

»Siyah!« she curred but the cat didn't show up. She had probably been fed up with waiting for her food and pushed off through the window, which was open just a crack, to catch a mouse in the garden. Apparently, self-reliance was the name of the game. She would put some food in her bowl anyway, just in case. Maybe she would want some later on.

But Julie set just one foot in the kitchen, then covered her mouth in terror and stumbled back out into the hallway backwards.

Every single knife that was to be found in the house – large knives and small knives, bread knives and vegetable knives, steak knives and poultry knives, everything that had a sharp blade – was lying on the kitchen counter in an orderly line and all knife points were pointing at her. Julie understood this warning only too well. There was no doubt. This was clearly a threat. Amie had sounded the bell for the next round and this time she was serious about it.

The sight of all those knives really scared Julie. She tore open every drawer and stuffed all the knives into them in no particular order just so she didn't have to see them anymore.

She gave a sigh of relief once they were all put away. She felt a little bit better already.

Julie decided to take a bath in the main bathroom. She needed to calm herself down and what better way to do this than a relaxing bath? She ran herself a bath and added a generous amount of lavender bath oil which she had found on a small table next to the bathtub. She gathered shower gel, shampoo and body lotion as well as a fluffy bath towel. She laid out the old hairdryer, too, having checked that it still worked. She then lit the candles placed on the window sill so that she could see them from the bath, as well as the beautiful old candlestick standing next to the bath oil. Then she undressed and lowered herself gently got into the bath.

It was heavenly! Julie closed her eyes, ducked under the water and stayed underwater as long as she could hold her breath. She didn't come up again until she ran out of oxygen. Just as she was wiping the foam from her eyes, she heard it. That whistling again, that tune. Within spitting distance.

»I'm here.« said a voice and Julie's eyes darted into the direction from which the words had come. Amie could not be overlooked. She was looking at her out of the ornate cheval mirror next to the window, just opposite the bathtub. And Amie looked exactly like herself, Julie. How was that even possible? Was she looking at her own reflection and only imagining the voice? No, of course not. That was impossible. She was sitting in the bathtub, after all, naked and dripping wet, while Amie was looking at her from the mirror, perfectly dry and fully dressed.

»What do you want? Why can't you just leave me in peace?« Julie asked miserably. She couldn't have explained why but Amie's deadpan face scared her. It really scared the shit out of her.

»I want out of here. Just let me out and I promise you will never see me again.« was Amie's unexpected response.

It had not occurred to Julie but now it was beginning to dawn on her.

»Wait a minute. YOU want out? You? This was all about you all the time? I thought you meant me, that I should get out, out of the house. But by *OUT* you really meant that YOU want out?!«

»About time you got it.« Amie replied, unmoved. »Took you long enough. Did you really think I care about you? I don't care about you at all. I just want out of here, that's all. I don't care about anything else and definitely not about you. You're just completely insane. You should see a psychologist!«

Those last two sentences pushed Julie's buttons.

»Shut it! Shut the fuck up!« she shrieked as loud as she could. »I am not insane! Is that clear? I AM NOT INSANE!«

She grabbed the first thing she could get a hold of – which happened to be the heavy old candlestick - and threw it into Amie's direction with all her might. It clashed and clanked when it hit its target and the mirror shattered into a million pieces.

»Thanks!« Amie smirked. »There you go! Now wasn't that easy?«

Julie saw Amie's grimace in one of the mirror shards. Amie waved at her, her arm actually sticking out of the broken fragment as she did so.

»Look!« said Amie, pointing at something. Julie obeyed and saw the hairdryer lying on the rim of the bathtub – with the plug in the socket!

NO!!!!!

Had she left it there? No, definitely not. She would never have done that. It must have been Amie.

»Bye, you crackpot!«, Amie laughed again.

Julie's eyes were glued to the hairdryer. Just as she leaned forward to move it to safety, she saw the hairdryer slip off the rim in slow motion and fall into the water.

Julie screamed… and it was over.

+++ BREAKING NEWS +++

The patient who went missing from the psychiatric clinic in Cardiff a couple of days ago was found dead in the bathtub of a decrepit house in a remote part of Wales. According to initial investigations, there are no suspicious circumstances surrounding the death. Allegedly, it was suicide by electrocution. The deceased had been in treatment in the clinic's high security ward for severe paranoid schizophrenia for years. It is still unclear how she was able to leave the clinic unnoticed and what relation she had to the derelict house. The clinic director had to step down following the scandal.